This Halloween Coloring Book Belongs To:

____

____

Book Title:

<BELOVED AUTUMN FESTIVITIES>
Coloring Halloween & Thanksgiving 4+

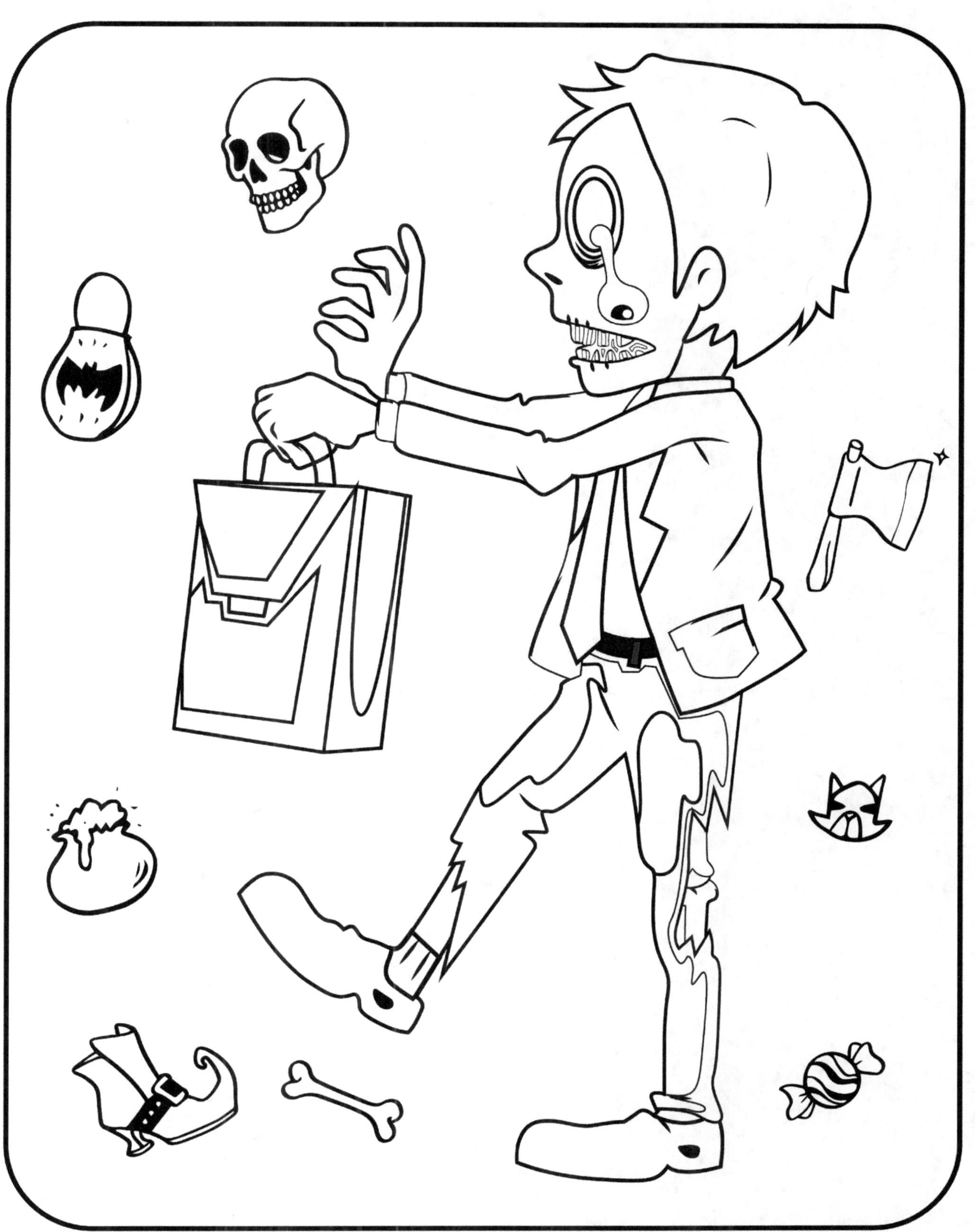

R.I.P

HAPPY
THANKS
GIVING

HAPPY
Thanks
giving

www.ingramcontent.com/pod-product-compliance
Lightning Source LLC
LaVergne TN
LVHW080815170826
845678LV00011B/2021
9798485461096